Vampire

(Vlad V Series)

By Mit Sandru

Chivileri Publishing

Table of Contents

Chapter 1

The subway was empty. As a young and fairly attractive woman, I tend to prefer a more crowded car, but the others were empty as well. I sat down and read the ads posted near the ceiling. At the next stop, a tall, white-haired, distinguished-looking gentleman entered the car. He did not sit down but, after staring at me for a moment, nodded politely. This guy was from another era, for sure. He was dressed in a black suit, with black cowboy boots and a black cape. Or maybe the cape was a trench coat; it was drizzling in New York City that night, and he wore it like a cape. On the other hand, he might have been a clergyman.

He held himself very erect and tall, almost regally. He did not hold on to any of the handlebars for support, even when the subway stopped rather abruptly. He had perfect balance. I saw him notice the book I was holding in my hand. It was one of the latest vampire books. I felt embarrassed and somehow uneasy – I was alone with a man who looked like, you know, a vampire, and I was holding a book about vampires.

I couldn't help but examine him – yes, examine him. His hair, as I said, was white, combed back, and he was as pale as a sheet of paper. I first thought he was an albino, but his eyebrows were salt-and-pepper dark. He had a narrow, straight nose, not too long, not too short. He was clean-shaven, and his lips were thin and purple – not red or pink, but purple. Could he have been one of the living dead? No, he didn't look like a corpse.

His black jacket was double-breasted, and a blood-red handkerchief protruded in a perfect triangle from his breast pocket. The rest of his outfit was normal, except for the black cowboy boots. What was up with that? A vampire in cowboy boots. He was tall, so he didn't need the added advantage of higher heels. Maybe it was, like, a fashion statement or something.

On his right ring finger, he wore an enormous and intricate gold ring. Walking at night with such a treasure was hazardous. As he raised his hand to smooth his hair, I observed a gold watch on his left wrist. This guy was for sure taking his chances, going around at night in Manhattan like that.

Deep black eyes looked back at me intently. He noticed me scanning him. After I had inspected him like a piece of merchandise, I decided to act more civilly. I smiled at him. He smiled back and showed his perfect teeth, except that he was missing his upper canines. You know – the pointy teeth on either side of the front incisor teeth. I guess Medicare doesn't cover all of a senior citizen's dental needs.

A New York City transit cop came into our car through the end door, doing his rounds to keep the subway safe. He walked nonchalantly; it was a slow evening, on Sunday at 9 pm. Neither the older gentleman nor I gave him cause for suspicion, so he was relaxed. We were very much the image of the law-abiding, responsible citizens politicians refer to in their speeches. The cop passed by, giving each of us a short nod as we exchanged glances with him. He moved on to the next car.

At the next stop, three young guys wearing chain-studded leather and weird Goth makeup saw me from the platform. Here I was, a cute girl in a skirt and raincoat, sitting delicately on the bench with her ankles crossed to the side, and they decided to run up along the train and enter my car. They made no bones about enjoying what they saw: me. But why me? I didn't give the appearance of a devil worshipper, or whatever they were. Oh, no! They're looking for a virgin to sacrifice tonight. I'm flattered – not!

I'm no snob, but I do have my standards. They were definitely not in my league, so I turned my head and looked away. Undeterred, two of them sat down on either side of me, while the third one stood in front of me. It was intimidating, and I reached for the mace can in my raincoat pocket. Just in case.

The old gentleman stepped right next to the guy in front of me, fixing him with a stony gaze. For some reason, that leather-and-chains-wearing guy felt the implied threat of his stare and never looked at the old man. It seemed to be a standoff. Those three couldn't just move away now without losing face. The other two guys sitting next to me shifted in their seats. I swore I could smell their perspiration, a nervous sweat. The subway finally stopped at the next station, and, as if relieved to see the doors open, the three of them bolted out of the subway car.

I looked up, but the old gentleman had moved away, back to the same spot he stood in before. He really intrigued me now. OK, I was little scared, too. Who was this man, and what were his intentions? What if he were to follow me home, which was now just three stops from here?

To my surprise, he exited at the next stop, 42nd Street. The stop at the station was longer than usual, so, on an impulse, I decided to follow him. Where was he going? I walked quickly to catch up with him, and, at the top of one flight of stairs, I saw him take the exit for 40th Street and Broadway. I ran for the stairs that led to the opposite side of the street, but when I got to the top and stepped onto the sidewalk, I couldn't spot him. The streets were deserted, except for some cars and yellow cabs. He had disappeared.

Chapter 2

Where could he have gone? Of course! He must have seen me following him, and he took the stairs back down into the subway station. He was letting me know who's in control. Oh, well! I had to get back to the subway to catch the next train home. As I turned to descend the stairs, from the corner of my eye, I saw him. He was sitting in a booth in a 24-hour café on my side of the street. He was watching me; he beckoned me in. I was caught. Curiosity killed the cat. That's funny, because my nickname is Cat.

Without hesitation – foolishly, you might say – I went in and joined him in the booth. There were two cups of steaming coffee on the table.

"I took the liberty of ordering you a decaf." He spoke with an accent that I thought sounded European, but not from Western Europe. "Allow me to introduce myself. My name is Vlad."

Oh, boy, he was a nut case, for sure, and I fell for it. Next, he was going to tell me his last name was "the Impaler."

I cleared my throat. "Nice to meet you. My name is Cat, and you didn't have to trouble with the coffee. I need to go. Tomorrow I have to get up early. It's Monday, you know."

"No trouble at all. And don't be frightened. A nut case, I'm not."

"What? What makes you say that?" I put on my most sincere face.

"Well, let's be realistic. I told you my name is Vlad, as in Vlad the Impaler. I speak with an accent, I dress unusually, and I am very pale. Who else could I be but a vampire? Hmm?"

He had disarmed me. "Yes. True. And here is a young chick with a vampire book, every young woman's dream, ready to be spellbound by a handsome and rich vampire, even a fake one."

"Like me?"

"Sorry, I didn't mean it that way." I am sure I blushed.

"That's all right. Only fakes would take it as an insult."

"You mean, fake vampires?"

"Most are fake vampires. It is a good way to get, as you said, young chicks, and the literature is full of this kind of rubbish." He pointed to my book. "Strong, good-looking man, rich beyond belief, living forever, and making love to you all night long."

I ignored the all-night-long part. "Of course, they are all fake vampires. This book and others like it are all fantasies." I needed to clarify that point. I was definitely not a ditz. I raised my cup to take a drink but stopped. What if he had put something in my coffee?

"I understand. You are definitely not a ditz."

I was so surprised that I dropped my cup, splattering coffee all over the table, my blouse, and even his jacket.

"I'm so sorry!" I grabbed a handful of napkins from the dispenser to blot my blouse. I grabbed another handful and reached to clean his jacket. He smiled. I did the best I could to get the coffee off him, but, you know, coffee on a black suit is hardly visible. I was surprised how firm his chest felt. This guy was no stranger to the gym.

"No need to apologize," he said calmly. He raised his hand. "Waitress, two fresh cups of coffee, please."

The plump, middle-aged waitress brought a pot of decaf coffee and two cups. She cleaned the mess and then filled our new cups. I saw her eyes shifting from him to me. Hey, this is New York – it's practically normal to see a couple like us having coffee.

I took a sip of my fresh, hot coffee that was now safe to drink. "Again, I'm really sorry about what happened." Why did he use the word "ditz"? It was as if he could read my mind. Strange. "May I ask you where you're from originally?"

He gave me a thin smile. "Ah, you detected my accent. I am from Transylvania."

"Uh-huh. That's a good one." I decided to be cheeky. "And you're Dracula." I felt ashamed as soon as I said that. He probably is told that by a lot of people.

"No, I am not Dracula." He didn't seem to be offended. "But I knew him."

I froze. Was he pulling my leg? He had to be joking. Let's see how far he'll go. "You knew Dracula? I thought Dracula was the stuff of fiction, a made-up character."

"True. I meant to say that I knew the man who inspired the legend and, later, the name Dracula and the book."

"Wasn't that centuries ago, when the real-life character lived? How could you have known him?"

"I'm related to him. He was my uncle."

Chapter 3

Good story. He got my attention. "Your great-great-great-uncle?"

"No. My uncle. By blood."

This was weird. He was related to Vlad the Impaler!

"I realize that it sounds weird, to be related to Vlad the Impaler, but it is true. You see, his name was Vlad, of the Draculesti family. My name is Vlad Draculesti, as well. My father, Radu, and he were brothers, but not of the same political allegiance." He sighed.

I propped my cheek on my hand, giving him my most disbelieving expression.

"All right, let me explain." He smiled. "I know it sounds unbelievable, but I am 300 years old. I was born in the year 1453, the year Constantinople fell to the Turks. I was born in Sighisoara, Transylvania. Lovely town, Sighisoara is. My uncle Vlad was born in 1431. He became king of Wallachia, which is south of Transylvania – all these areas are now in Romania. As a king, he fought for independence from the Ottoman Empire, the Turks. I joined him eagerly in battles against the pagans. Shamefully, my father – his brother– was on the side of the Turks.

"We terrified the Turks with night raids, killing many. Sultan Mehmed II became so fearful of my uncle that he put a big prize on his head. By then, we were already vampires. It is not easy killing a vampire. But traitors managed to behead him while he was asleep. They took his head in a jar of honey to Constantinople – Istanbul today – as proof that he was dead and as a trophy."

"You know your history well," I said.

"I lived it."

"Sorry, but that's hard to believe. No one lives that long."

"Vampires do."

"OK, let's leave it at that. How did you become a vampire?"

"My uncle and I were infected. We became vampires while we were detained as prisoners. I suspect there was a virus that we caught, and it transformed us into vampires. Probably that's what convinced Corvinus, the king of Hungary, to free us from the prison in Transylvania."

"Virus? You mean you weren't bitten by other vampires?" This was kind of news to me, but plausible. Why not a virus?

"Back then we didn't know what transformed us. With the knowledge provided by modern science nowadays, I suspect it was a virus. However, no one had bitten us. We bit others afterward, that's true."

"How did you catch the virus? A mosquito bite?"

"Not at all. This is how it happened. In the last year of our captivity, my uncle and I were moved deeper underground into some forgotten cell that hadn't been occupied by prisoners in decades. It was cold and damp down there, with no daylight. My uncle and I had to find our way around in total darkness. The only time we saw light was when the guard came down with a torch to bring us bread and water, once a day.

"After a month down there, both of us caught the plague. That's what we thought. We

19

had very high fevers and assumed we would die soon. The plagues decimated Europe during those times. The guard stopped visiting us, afraid that he might catch the illness. After a week the fever broke, and we returned to normal. We called to the guard to bring us food and water. It was not until the guard came down with his torch that we realized we could see in the dark. Actually, it was after he left. It was as if that light from the flame ignited our ability to see in complete darkness.

"We were surprised at first, but we liked it. We could see. The next problem was that the bread and water did not taste good, no matter how hungry we were. We craved meat. There were rats down there, but we could never see to catch them before. Now we could not only see them but catch them with little effort. We figured that the rats we caught had to be the lazy ones, for it was so easy for us to snag them.

"We tried to eat their flesh, but we didn't like it. What we liked better was the blood. It was somehow satisfying. We lived for a while on rat blood, gaining back some of our strength. As for the bread and water, we never touched them again. Oh, my goodness, your cup is empty!"

I had drunk all the coffee, completely absorbed by his story.

"Waitress, a coffee refill, please!"

I observed that he hadn't drunk any of his coffee. The same waitress came over and refilled my cup. "Would you like anything else?" she asked.

"Would you like a pastry, a piece of pie with that coffee?" Vlad asked me.

I shook my head.

"Please, would you bring a slice of pie and a pastry? Just in case the young lady changes her mind."

"Sure thing, sir. How about your coffee? Need a refresh?" she asked.

"That would be wonderful."

She returned with the two dishes and a fresh cup of coffee.

"You were surviving on rat blood. That's the last thing you said."

"Oh, yes. But it was not entirely nourishing. However, when the guard came down once a day, we found his smell to be very attractive. Before our fever, the man had stunk something awful, as if he hadn't bathed in years, which he hadn't. We figured that he must smell the same as before. The alluring smell was his blood.

"The next day, we lured him to the bars for a chat and grabbed him. My uncle opened his jugular with the famous vampire bite. I took my turn. His blood felt like pure life energy flowing into my body. We debated whether to suck him dry or leave him just a bit drained, so we could drink some more another day. We were satisfied, so we let him go. He left on wobbly legs without saying a word."

"But didn't he remember what happened or notice later the punctures on his neck?"

"We were concerned about that, but the two holes caused by my uncle's canine teeth closed quickly, leaving only two blue bruises – two hickeys, as you young people might say. After we let go of him, he slid down to the floor. At first, we thought we had killed him. I reached through the bars and slapped him. He woke up; he had just been sleeping. After he woke, he said nothing. He simply departed on wobbly legs."

"But didn't you infect him with your bites?"

"That's a legend. If that were the case, there would be more vampires than humans in this world. There was no infection. He stayed human and provided us with fresh nourishing blood for months to come. We gave him the rat meat to keep him fed and healthy. He appreciated that."

"I don't get it. You're saying that you cannot infect your victims?" I reached for the pastry.

"Well, I don't know for sure. Remember, we were infected in that cell without being bitten. I presume that I could infect others – after all, I have the virus in me, but it has never happened, as far as I know. However, I have met, on rare occasions, other vampires, both men and women."

"You did? There are others like you?"

"Yes, but we don't keep in touch, much. We are lonely creatures. Of the night."

"How do you know it was a virus that infected you?" I finished my pastry and offered him the plate with the pie.

He shook his head. "No, thank you, the pie is yours. How do I know it was a virus? Well, as I said, I've met other vampires. And I inquired how they got to be that way. None remembered being bitten, but they recalled contracting the ability through a high fever, followed by the same symptoms I experienced. And none of the others ever visited or were even near the place where my uncle and I became vampires."

I pulled the pie close to me. I looked doubtful about what he had just said.

He continued. "I know it was a virus. I've researched all my life for the answer. You see, two hundred years after I became a vampire, I returned to the ruins of the prison in Transylvania. It was near the Hunyad Castle. In Romania, it is known as Castelul Hunedoara. The underground tunnels were more or less passable. I reached the cell where we became vampires, and I found a vaulted crypt underneath the floor – "

"Who was in it?"

"Not who, but what."

"OK, what?"

"It was a creature. The closest thing I can associate it with is the devil."

Chapter 4

"The devil! Oh, my God!" I crossed myself like a good Catholic girl. "What did it look like?"

"Like the devil." Vlad saw by my expression that I wanted more details, so he continued. "In the crypt I found a stone sarcophagus. It was massive, the biggest sarcophagus I've ever seen. And I've seen a few. The lid was three feet thick. Even I had difficultly pushing over that lid and opening the box."

"Why was it so heavy?"

"To keep whatever was interred in it inside. In the box I found another sarcophagus. This one was made of lead."

"Lead?"

"Yes, lead. Inches thick. It had an intricate latching mechanism, but I managed to unlatch it and open the heavy cover. I expected to find a mummy. Instead, there was only a skeleton with some gelatinous material around it, like a dark-blue gel. Although the skeleton resembled that of a human, it was not human. It had a tail, like a lizard. The legs and feet were those of an animal, like the hind legs of a velociraptor. It had a pair of arms and hands with long fingers and claws. What was most curious, though, was that it had a pair of wing bones, for wings like those of a bat. The head was elongated, and it had a pair of horns. The jaw and teeth were definitely those of a carnivore, with big canines. It was the devil."

"Wow! You tell a good story."

"It is not a story. It is the truth."

"OK. So what happened next? How about the gooey stuff?" I took a bite of the pie. This disgusting story was making me hungry.

"The gooey stuff, as you call it, might have been the remains of its flesh. That's where the virus came from. I had it analyzed twenty years ago. Nasty stuff. Anyway, when I opened the grave, I exposed the virus. It could have infected Transylvania, maybe all of Romania and its neighboring countries. I didn't want this to happen to others, to make Transylvania a hot bed of vampirism. I closed the lead box and the sarcophagus. I went back with several barrels of gunpowder and destroyed the tunnels to bury the grave forever."

"Don't you think that archaeologists will dig one day and find it?"

"They might, but today there is a nice church built on top of it. No one will dig underneath it for a long time."

"How convenient."

"I funded the building of that church in the 1820s. Churches tend to stand for centuries. Unless you have a madman like Stalin, who wanted to destroy religion by demolishing churches. Anyway, it's all safe now."

"That's good. Humanity has nothing to fear. Now, back to when you just became a vampire – how did you get out of that prison?"

"The guard's blood nourished us, and we became true vampires, strong and quick. One day I tried my hand at those thick bars on our jail cell, and I snapped them like twigs. We decided to pay a visit to our good old King Corvinus, who happened to be at the Hunyad Castle. We surprised him at dinner. He soiled his garments when he saw us; it ruined his appetite, too. On the spur of the moment, he decided to allow my uncle Vlad to return to Wallachia to recapture his throne and fight the

Turks. He gave us an army, to boot. But it didn't last long, and my uncle was killed." He looked outside as if remembering that tragic time.

"Sorry about that." I took another bite of my pie.

"Well, as they say, that's life. Look at the time. Aren't you supposed to return home? Tomorrow is Monday." He pointed to his gold watch. It was 10:30 pm.

I smiled. He had used my excuse to end this conversation. "As I said, you tell a good story. You can't stop now."

"But that was it. There is no more."

"Can I ask you more questions?"

"If it's not too late for you, go ahead."

"Is it true that you sleep in a coffin?"

"I'm not dead. A comfortable bed, a firm bed, is what I sleep in."

"So you don't sleep in dirt or a coffin?"

"Do you?"

"Sorry, it's all that legend stuff, I guess. How about sunlight?"

"Oh, yes. The sunlight. No, I don't die in sunlight. I don't turn to ashes. The sunlight affects my eyes, though. It's too bright."

"So you can be outdoors during the day, in full sunlight?"

"Sure, but I have to wear sunglasses. Like these." He reached in his pocket and pulled out a dark pair of sunglasses with side shields.

I reached over, and he gave them to me. I tried them on. I could hardly see anything through them. "These are really dark. Are you a nocturnal person?"

"Yes, I prefer the night. I sleep during the day. Besides, if I am out during the day, people stare at me. I am so white that I stick out like a sore thumb."

I thought he might be afflicted by vitiligo. "Yeah, I see your predicament. So you only eat or drink blood?"

"Yes, anything else doesn't taste appetizing."

"This I find hard to believe, Vlad. How many gallons of blood per day do you need to live on? Are you alive at all?"

31

"I am talking to you, am I not? Yes, I'm alive. A different kind of alive. As for blood, it doesn't take that much for me to be energized."

"How come? Here it's been almost two hours, and I ate the pastry and the pie, drank two cups of coffee, and soon I'll be hungry again. How can you survive on a liquid diet?"

"Maybe because I'm not human anymore."

Chapter 5

I got chills up my back. Who am I conversing with here? "What do you mean?"

"The skeleton I found buried under the cell, whatever that was, it was not human. I am pretty sure that it was a blood drinker as well. I became it, although I maintained my human body. Here, feel this." He extended his hand and covered mine.

It was cold and hard. I felt as if a marble statue was touching me. I clasped his hand with both of mine and inspected it closely. It was white with blue veins and very firm. I flexed his fingers, and they worked perfectly. I just could not imagine how such hard muscles – if they were muscles – could flex as easily as they did. "Are you made of flesh? Do you have blood in your veins?"

He looked at me thoughtfully. "I am not sure if I am made of human flesh. I think my flesh has been plasticized. Probably similar to plastination. That's the closest explanation I can give you. As for blood, I don't have blood flowing in my veins. My veins are filled with a viscous substance, like the gel I told you I found with the skeleton. And it is blue in color. I am more like a reptile, having the same temperature as the ambient air. But, unlike reptiles, cold does not bother me."

"Can you be cut?"

"Try it." He seemed amused.

There was a cutlery set wrapped in a white napkin on the table. I unwrapped it and removed the serrated knife, which would have had trouble cutting an apple. Nevertheless, I laid the knife on his open palm. "Are you sure?" He nodded. But wait, if I cut him, he might sue me. I'll take the chance. This is the moment of truth. Let's see if he bleeds.

I pulled the knife on his palm. Not a scratch. I tried again with more pressure. Not a dent. I placed my hand on the backside of the knife and pulled while pressing as hard as I could to cut him. I expected blood to squirt out. Nothing.

This was ridiculous. I thought he was probably wearing a special-material glove. I rolled up his sleeve, but there was no glove. I saw his wrist with blue veins in it.

I placed the knife on his wrist and began sawing with the knife. At that moment, the waitress came to see if we needed anything else. When she saw me running the knife back and forth like a saw over his wrist, she squealed. Luckily, she didn't drop the coffee pot.

I jumped, holding the knife up.

"What are you doing?" Her eyes were the size of plates.

"No need to be alarmed," said Vlad. "See." He raised his wrist to show her his uninjured skin. "Not a scratch. We were trying to find out how dull your knives are. They are dull."

I nodded dumbly. There was no trace or any mark on his wrist. The waitress turned abruptly and left. "I think she'll be calling the cops," I said, looking in her direction. "Let's go." I pulled my wallet out and opened it. "How much do I owe you?"

"Nothing. It is on me." He went to the cashier and paid.

I waited outside for him, puzzled and intrigued. "We can't scare the civilians," I said as he came out. "As if I am not a civilian as well." I burst out laughing.

He laughed as well. "That's a good one."

"How come I couldn't cut you?"

"The knife was dull. I can be cut, albeit with a sharper object and more effort. Would you like me to wave down a cab for you?"

It was just before midnight, and I was sure I could take the subway, even at this hour. "No. I'll go by subway."

"In that case, let me escort you. Just in case."

"A perfect gentleman."

Just as I said that, from behind us I heard someone say, "Don't move, grandpa. We have a gun. You and the chick, turn around real slow. Give us your wallets. The ring and the watch, too."

We both turned slowly, as he ordered. My teeth were chattering from fear. Two dark men, one holding a gun, looked menacingly at us. We were easy targets, an old man and a girl.

And the old man was wearing gold jewelry. It was a good heist.

Before I could object, Vlad stepped in front of me. With lightening speed, he pushed the two men toward the alley's dead end. I clearly saw them flying backward in a vertical position, until they crashed into the wall at the end of the alley, twenty or more feet away. They didn't get up or make a sound.

"Uh-h-h," I managed to say. What just happened? Those two flew in the air as if they were on a conveyor belt. At high speed, too.

"Let's go. I'll get you a cab." He held my elbow and escorted me to the avenue. "Victims don't have rights anymore, only criminals. We better disappear before those two are found by someone or the police."

I was speechless and did as he instructed. He hailed down a cab, and I got in, as if in a dream. I heard him telling the driver my address, and he gave the cabby two $20 bills. He shut the door, and the cab took off.

I got to my apartment and crashed into bed.

Chapter 6

I woke up the next day just as I had collapsed into bed the night before: face down, with all my clothes on, even my raincoat and shoes. I hadn't even removed my make up or brushed my teeth. I sat up quickly when a thought crossed my mind: Did that guy, Vlad, slip me a tranquilizer or a date-rape drug? I didn't feel drowsy. I lifted my skirt; everything seemed to be in order there.

So why did I pass out so soundly? Information overload? Let's face it – you don't meet a charming fellow and a perfect gentleman who could be your grandfather, but who looks like Dracula, sans canine teeth, every day. And then he protects the damsel in distress – me – by shoving two hoodlums across an alleyway like two sacks of Styrofoam peanuts, and then he puts her in a cab and sends her home to safety. And he buys her coffee and pastry and pie and pays her cab fare, too.

The story was too incredible. I wish I'd recorded what he said. It would make a great book, if it were true. Wake up, Cat! He's a swindler, a conman. If he didn't try to get into my pants – provided he could get it up – he was after my money and my iPad. Except that I only have next month's rent in my checking account, and no savings.

What was he after? A young chick? Did I look that desperate? I didn't think so.

I got up from the bed and ran to the door to check the latch. I was safe. I looked at the clock. Damn! I needed to be at work in five minutes. Work is the curse of the drinking man, like my dad used to say. Except I'm not a man or a drinker. I better call in sick. There goes my reputation, calling in sick on Monday: "God knows what she did the whole weekend!" That's what those bitches in the office will gossip about.

What if I told them the truth? I met a vampire. No, that's not a good idea. Next they'll ask me if he looks like Brad Pitt or Tom Cruise. No imagination there. I could call and tell my boss I'll be late. No, I don't think I'll be able to concentrate today. I'll call in sick.

Taking a shower didn't clear my mind, although I felt clean and refreshed. With a towel wrapped around my head, I looked in the mirror and shouted, "What the hell is going on?" Oops, my mom would have not approved. I looked up. "Sorry, mom." I know she and my dad are up there in heaven.

I dressed in blue jeans and a t-shirt. Why did he tell me all that stuff? If he lied and made up the story, he's after something and he is a crook. But he let me go. Maybe last night was not a good time for him to do whatever he wanted to do. He was all dressed in black. Oh, my God! He's a serial killer! That's it. A cold-blooded, calculating killer. Who knows how many defenseless women he's killed. And he knows my address. He told the cabby where to take me.

The door intercom buzzed. I jumped. I stared, dumbstruck, at the intercom, which buzzed again. I walked to it and pressed the button. "Who is it?"

"Delivery from Amici Bakery."

"What kind of delivery?"

"Croissants, pastries, a cappuccino, and freshly squeezed orange juice."

"Are you sure it's for me?"

"Is your name Cat?"

I hesitated. "I didn't order that."

"Someone did. It is all paid for. Come on, lady, it's free. Even the tip was paid."

Croissants, pastries, a cappuccino, and freshly squeezed orange juice sounded just about perfect. But who paid for them? Who else but Vlad. Oh, what the heck. "I'll come down. Thanks!" I grabbed my keys and took the elevator to the building's foyer.

A Latino guy was holding a big white bag with the bakery logo on it. I opened the door. "Do you know who ordered this?"

The guy shook his head. "No, it was ordered online."

"No one else touched the contents except you guys?"

"No. Of course not."

I took the bag, thanked him, and, after I closed the entrance door, I opened it. Yes, just like he said. Enough breakfast to last me for a week.

Back in my apartment, I enjoyed the cappuccino and a croissant. Is this the romantic approach? He didn't send me flowers, just breakfast. He's too old. If he's not a killer, what else could he be? I have no money. Does he want my ID, my password to Facebook? That's too much effort just to get my identity information. Besides, he probably knows everything there is to know about me already. He's likely watching me from across the street with binoculars. I went to the window and pulled the shade down.

On the other hand, what if he is who he says he is: a vampire. Let's think this through realistically. There's no such thing as vampires. There are no extraterrestrials, either. Well, maybe ET exists. And if Vlad is a vampire, he drinks human blood. He is a parasite, no different than a mosquito, a flea, or a leech. I shuddered. But he said he doesn't kill his victims or infect them to change them into vampires.

It's hard to believe that I'm thinking about this. It would be fascinating if it were true. You're slipping, Cat! He is a new kind of predator. I'm confused. Wait a second; let's check him out.

I Googled him and found people named as such, most of them in Central Europe. Some even have Facebook pages. All in all, what I found were common people with that name or young punks trying to act tough. No sign of the older gentleman I met last night who bought me breakfast this morning.

Evening came. Even after all that heavy thinking, I still had no answers. Then my cellphone rang. "Hello?"

"Good evening, Cat," Vlad said. "I hope you liked the breakfast."

Chapter 7

"Are you after my blood? Are you fattening me up to eat me?"

"What silly ideas! If I need blood, I hit a blood bank. Blood is abundant, and it comes in easy-to-store plastic bags. Durable, too."

I smiled. He was funny. "OK, Vlad, what do you want? You know my address and my cellphone number. What do you want?"

"Remember, Cat, you followed me, not the other way around."

"OK, can I say good-bye now? Just one more thing: How did you know my address last night?"

"I saw your address when you opened your wallet at the café. As for the good-bye, we can part company, but if I recall, last night you were curious to know more about me, while trying to slash my wrist."

"Yes, I was. But you said that's all there was." I was pacing around.

"As far as how I became a vampire, yes."

"Well, that's good enough for me. Thanks for everything. Good-bye!" I pushed the off button on my cell.

"Damn!" I called back his number. "You mean there is more?"

"As much as you want to know. Cat, I'll be honest. I like you, but I'm not interested in your blood, or in romancing you, or killing you. I am a loner, and, occasionally, when I meet someone interesting, I like to talk. That's all."

"And after you tell me all your secrets, you'll kill me?"

"You are the first one in a long time to whom I've revealed what I really am. I didn't kill any of them."

I thought about what he said. I was so unsure, undecided about what to do. But then, I didn't feel threatened by him. "Do you want to talk?"

"Would you like to take a stroll?"

"Yes."

"On the other hand, do you have an appetite for dinner?"

"Yes."

"Do you like Italian?"

"Yes."

"Do you know Ristorante Napoli on 46th?"

"Yes."

"I'll meet you there in an hour?"

"Yes." I found I could say only "yes" to whatever he asked me.

He hung up.

I arrived there an hour later. The restaurant was not far from my apartment. I was dressed for action: boots, jeans, and a leather jacket. I slipped a switchblade in my boot. Yes, I have one of those, and mace in my pocket – a girl can't be too careful in the big city.

Vlad was waiting for me in a maroon-leather booth. He had already ordered a bottle of Chianti.

He stood up. "Good evening, Cat. You look lovely tonight." He was dressed in a black silk jacket, black shirt and pants, and his black cowboy boots.

"I bet you say that to all your women," I said as I sat down in the booth.

He smiled. "Vino?"

I nodded, and he filled my glass. His was already full. "If you don't eat, why go to restaurants?"

"I like wine." He lifted his glass. "*Salute.*"

I raised my glass. "Cheers. How come you drink wine?"

"This answer may surprise you: Alcohol is my fuel."

"I don't understand."

"You eat food for energy; I drink alcohol. And wine has alcohol, so that's why I consume it."

"That makes sense. And the wine is red. But how about the blood drinking?"

The waiter brought a basket of mini-baguettes and went through his routine. I ordered the house special just to get rid of him. Vlad did not order food.

"Yes, the blood. Why do you think vampires drink human blood?"

"I don't know – for food, to kill?" I shrugged and took a bite from my baguette.

"It seems that's what people believe – that we drink blood for food and that we do it to strike fear in humans. That is not true. I drink human blood to live. Human blood, and all other animal blood, has energy. Life energy. I need the blood to stay alive. Without it, I would die. And, as I said, instead of consuming food for energy in order to be animated, we, I drink alcohol. Alcohol for us is like gasoline for a car. But I never get drunk. "

"For nutritional purposes? That's news to me. Then why don't you drink animal blood and stop vampiring on humans?"

"Human blood is the richest. I have to drink the blood from an entire goat to equal two ounces of human blood."

"Really? That little! How often do you need to drink?"

"Once a week."

"Then why do we think you are a threat to us?"

"You tell me. Maybe the vampire-story writers and movie makers made it so."

"But you still kill people." I took a drink of my wine and observed him over the rim of the glass.

"I can kill, just like the next man. And I've killed in my life, in war, or to defend myself. But I never killed anyone to drink her blood or just for the fun of it."

That made me feel better. I don't know why. I'm such a romantic. Wake up, stupid, I slapped myself mentally. "You said *her* blood. You drink women's blood only?"

"Or men's. It doesn't matter, although I prefer women. Maybe because it's sexually arousing."

"Aha." Sexually arousing for whom? Better leave the subject alone. "Where do you get your blood nowadays?" I kind of expected for him to reach across the table and sink his teeth into my neck. Don't fear, Cat – he is toothless.

"The blood bank," he said matter-of-factly.

"You weren't kidding," I said, taken aback. "Why?"

He sighed. He lifted his upper lip with two fingers to show me the missing canine teeth. "You see? I have no canines, no fangs. I cannot bite."

"So you have to resort to blood donated to the blood bank by innocent donors."

"Yes. I could cut someone with a blade and drink their blood, but it is so uncivilized, and it will cause the villagers to come after me with torches, clubs, pitch-forks, and rakes."

Funny. "Has that happened to you?"

"Oh, yes. On a few occasions, in the old country, a long time ago."

"So you are from Transylvania. Why do you live in New York City?"

"It is a good place to maintain anonymity. Since I live so long, I would raise suspicions with the locals in smaller places. That's why I left Transylvania and lived in many other places, all over the world. Big cities are best.

You can get lost in the crowd. No one knows you."

"I suppose you have a place here in Manhattan." I was nosy, but what the heck.

"Yes, I have my own place on the Upper East Side. Even a vampire needs a place to rest." Vlad winked at me.

"You dog! Is that where you take your lady friends?"

"Oh, it is not like that. Vampires don't reproduce. Our sexual organs function very well, but my libido is very low. It must be my age."

"You mean to say that you've never had amorous affairs?"

"As a vampire, sure I have. But it was better before I became a vampire. For a human, the satisfaction and pleasure is a lot better."

"You've now ruined all my fantasies about vampires," I chuckled.

"That doesn't mean I cannot fall in love, or don't enjoy a lady's company, or am not able to offer a lady the most unforgettable night of her life."

"Do you suck her blood when you make love to a woman?"

"I used to. That's what makes them ecstatic."

I blushed, but luckily the food arrived, and I was saved. After it was in front of me, I decided, before I ate, to ask him one more question. "Do vampire age?"

Chapter 8

He took a drink of wine and pondered how to answer my question. "No, they don't age. Of course, I am old-looking, and I wasn't old when I became a vampire. Begin eating, and I will tell you a secret no one would ever guess."

I took a bite and listened attentively.

"When I became a vampire in that forsaken cell, I was only 23 years old. I was a young man, and I stayed that way for hundreds of years. Among all the other changes in my body, my canine teeth started growing. Not too long, mind you. It would not scare anyone if they saw me laughing. However, the canines were different. For one, they retracted into the gum when not in use. When I bit someone, they grew long, coming out of their sheathing."

I stopped eating. I envisioned tiger fangs.

"The other characteristic of my canines was the venom."

I froze. I envisioned snake fangs.

"Not like snake venom, but vampire venom. It seals the punctures to prevent the victim from bleeding to death. It acts as a painkiller, amnesia inducer, and sedative. That's why a victim does not suffer, doesn't die, and does not remember what happened afterward. However, the most significant part of the venom is the ability to keep vampires forever young. By drinking human blood mixed with the venom, we never age."

"Wow! Then what happened to you?"

"Yes, yes, I aged." He took a moment and sipped his wine. "This is my shameful secret. It was in the 1960s, and I was having the time of my life. For some reason, all that sexual liberation made the young women so much more appetizing. I met a gal who intrigued me, and I even fell mildly in love with her. Yes, I was drinking her blood, and she thought she was getting hickeys from me.

"It was a minor inconvenience, considering the love making was pure ecstasy, she assured me. One day, after I had made love to her, I decided to tell her the truth about who I was. Big mistake. Instead of finding it cool, she was turned off. I got close to kiss her, and she butted me with her head and broke my left canine."

"Oh, my goodness!"

"I don't typically experience pain as a vampire, but when that happened, when my canine broke, it was painful – as painful as having a root canal without anesthetics, from what I've heard. That was the most painful experience I ever had as a vampire.

"I didn't realize the full extent of the damage at that time. She used my momentary incapacity to try to run away, but I caught her at the door. She was hysterical. She turned and hit me with her elbow in my right canine. She broke that one, too."

"No!" I was feeling sorry for him.

"I collapsed on the floor in agonizing pain. It took me a week to recover. I couldn't bite and energize myself with fresh blood. I resorted to taking advantage of junkies, bleeding them. Eventually, I figured out how to get blood through other means. But, after 500-plus years of staying young, I began to age. And I've aged ever since."

"I'm so sorry. Did you ever see that girl again?"

"Sadly, yes. I wanted to kill her for what she had done to me, but I couldn't find her. Ultimately, my fury subsided, and my thoughts of killing her evaporated. Twenty years later, I met her by chance, at night, in the streets of San Francisco. She was all drugged up. By then, I had aged twenty years, but she had aged forty. She looked haggard and decrepit. Drugs do that to you."

"Then what happened?"

"I took her to a rehab center. Drug addiction was the least of her problems. She had shared needles with other junkies and she contracted HIV, then known as AIDS. She died six month later."

"How many people have you told that you're a vampire?"

"Besides her? Just one woman in France during the French Revolution. I married her, and we lived together until she died in her fifties. When she died, she told me that I was the love of her life." Vlad stopped. It seemed that he was about to cry, but he recovered quickly. "That's the price you have to pay when you're immortal." He looked away.

A thought occurred to me. "Vlad, I am now only the third person you've ever told about your condition. Why?"

"Yes, there is a reason. But for that you need to visit my apartment."

Chapter 9

"Ha, ha, ha! You are good. You are so very good. I believed you. Very moving story, and now you want me to come with you to your lair, to close the deal." I folded my arms and shook my head, smiling bitterly.

"I've told you the truth," he said.

"But I don't buy it."

"I'm dying."

"Vampires die? That's news to me." I had my hand on the mace can, just in case.

The maître d stopped by our booth. "Vlad, why are you so sad?" he inquired. "Some more wine?" He refilled our glasses. "By the way, Charlie D'Aggio wants to meet you."

"D'Aggio, the baseball player?" I was surprised.

"The one and only. He wants a picture with you, just like the one with Joe DiMaggio." He pointed at the celebrity pictures on the walls. "Of course, here in our restaurant. Would you like a picture with this lovely young lady?"

Vlad shook his head.

"I would love a picture with Vlad," I said eagerly. "But with one condition."

Vlad looked at me quizzically.

"What would that condition be?" the maître d asked.

"That you put our picture on the wall."

"No problem. I hang all Vlad's pictures on our walls." He pulled out his digital camera and snapped a shot of us.

I smiled as graciously as I could muster under the circumstances. "Thank you! Could you print it and post it right now?" I asked.

"But of course." He left to get the picture printed. Monday was a slow night.

I turned back to Vlad. "I thought you were a loner."

"I am, but I cannot help if I come across as interesting to people and they want to chat with me. There are quite a few pictures of me on the walls here."

I took the hint, and I went perusing the photos. There he was: a younger Vlad with Joe DiMaggio. I spotted another picture of an older Vlad with Mayor Ed Koch. I guess he's known a lot of famous people, all of them dead. No, wait, I was wrong; there's a picture of him with Mayor Bloomberg. Hmm! I was having second thoughts about Vlad.

I sat down back at the table. Vlad seemed to be unperturbed. "Famous, aren't you?"

"I have a reputation as some kind of history expert."

The maître d returned and showed us the framed picture. "Even more famous, now that he's had his picture taken with you, young lady," he said after he hung the photo near our booth.

"Thanks! That was fast. I think I will be a celebrity now. Vlad and Cat."

"Our pleasure, Cat. Anything else?"

"No, I think we're ready to go," I said. "Vlad has something important to show me over at his place." Yes, I decided to take him up on his offer. After all, this way I had witnesses that I was with him and that I went with him to his apartment.

The maître d grinned knowingly. "Have an enchanting evening." He smiled and departed, as if leaving behind a dirty old man and a young chick.

"Why did you change your mind?" Vlad asked.

"Why are you dying?"

"I told you I'm aging, and when you get old enough, you die."

"You have many more years ahead of you."

"Not that much time."

"Is this a coincidence that we met, or did you plan this?" I was eager to hear what he had to say.

"It was a coincidence. When I saw you in the subway, I had a strong feeling about who you might be."

We arrived at his apartment in his private elevator. His place occupied the entire floor, and it had a breathtaking view of Central Park. He must be loaded; a pad like this costs millions. Judging by the many fine furniture pieces, and oil paintings on the wall, he had money to spare on expensive art, as well.

"OK, we're here," I said after a quick look around. "Are you going to kill me and drink my blood after all?"

He looked amused. "No, none of that. The restaurant has a picture of us. If I harm you, they'll catch me and throw me in the dungeon."

"Good! We understand each other then. I also texted all my friends and posted on Facebook about my visit here when I was in the ladies' room."

Vlad laughed heartedly. "Smart!" He took me by the elbow to his plush office. "This is what I wanted to show you." On the wall in front of his desk was an oil painting, lit by soft track lights. It was the portrait of a young woman.

The woman was me.

Chapter 10

I turned to him. "What's the meaning of this? Is this some kind of a joke?"

"No, that's not a joke. And that lady is not you."

"Then who?"

"Her name is Elena. She was my wife when I was human."

I covered my mouth with my hands. I couldn't help it – I was shocked. She was beautiful and so radiant, so alive. "Was – I mean – is Elena my ancestor?"

"Yes. She is your great-great-great-grandmother. I am sure there are probably more 'greats' that belong there than I mentioned."

"Tell me about her." I sat down on the sofa, keeping my eyes on her portrait.

"We married when I was seventeen. As was the custom back then among royalty and nobility, the marriage was arranged. I fell in love with her the first time I saw her. She loved me, too. She was fifteen. In time, we had a daughter. We were happy. I was a father, and we were going to try for more children, for sons.

"But soon I had to leave. My duty was to keep the Turks south of the Carpathians, after we failed to keep them south of the Danube. I was fighting with other like-minded young men from Wallachia, Moldavia, and Transylvania.

"But let me go back in time. When they were young, my father, Radu, and my uncle, Vlad, were taken to Constantinople as insurance against my grandfather, King Vlad II, rising against the Turks. My father grew to like Sultan Mehmed II and obeyed him. He fought for the Sultan against the Wallachians, his own people. I didn't see much of him when I was growing up in Transylvania. He was at Mehmed's court. My uncle, after becoming King Vlad III of Wallachia – also known as Vlad the Impaler – was a patriot. He broke with Mehmed and fought against the Ottoman Empire.

"I wanted to be like my uncle Vlad. He was my role model. When I was nine, he was forced into exile in Transylvania, and my father, Radu, became the Ottoman puppet king of Wallachia. Then I married beautiful Elena, after which I joined the fighters in Moldavia and Transylvania fighting against the Turks and my father. When I was in Transylvania in 1474, Vlad fell on bad terms with King Corvinus, and he was thrown in prison. I was arrested as well, and that's how I joined Vlad in prison and we became vampires.

"My father died in 1475. During that time, my wife was at his court with our daughter, Anina. Soon after we were released from King Corvinus' prison, Turkish assassins killed my wife as punishment for my joining Vlad III and helping him regain his throne in Wallachia. Elena was dead, and I was a vampire. I couldn't have any more children.

"I consoled myself by fighting for King Vlad III, Vlad the Impaler, against the Turks. I killed many. My uncle Vlad and I resumed his favorite night raids into the Turks' camps. We were vampires, so we were able to kill ten times as many Turks as before. In spite of our just fight, the Turks managed to assassinate Vlad, and all was over.

"I didn't know the fate of Anina until I escaped to Transylvania. Another relative adopted her. I provided for them and, when Anina was of age, we married her to a Saxon nobleman. Her family grew, and some descendants migrated as far as Germany and France. I lost track of them during the turmoil of the French Revolution and the Napoleonic wars. Until last night, when I saw you, I never thought I would meet any of my descendants." Vlad looked at Elena's portrait with loving eyes.

"You are my many-generations-ago grandfather. Are you sure I am your blood relative?"

"I researched you last night. Your lineage comes through Germany, then the US. Anina is your only Romanian ancestor. After that, you have German, French, Irish, and English ancestry. You came a long way for us to meet. Your mother was our blood relative. In my search I found out about your parents' death in the car accident. I'm sorry."

"Yes, I miss them."

He hugged me.

70

"Why didn't you become king of Wallachia?" I asked.

"It wasn't in me." He sighed. "I was asked, but I had a secret – I was a vampire. I preferred to slowly vanish."

"Was it true that King Vlad III was cruel and impaled his enemies?"

"My uncle told me that he was seven when he first killed a man, a prisoner. He had to. It was a rite of passage, part of his education at the Ottoman court. Besides the education he received at Sultan Mehmed's court, he was instructed in military matters and even in torture techniques.

"His father, King Vlad II, had been killed by the Turks – they stripped the skin off his face while he was alive. It was a cruel world. My uncle had to be cruel to stay alive. And, yes, he did impale many people. His enemies were terrified of him, and he was able to prevent more wars upon Wallachia and rebuild that land. He was just, too. Wallachia became a functioning kingdom rather than a ravaged country, vulnerable to pillaging by boyars and Turks alike.

"Yes, he was cruel with his enemies and with traitors. Unfortunately, only that aspect survived to be told today. But he was more than that."

"I'm sure he was," I said, impressed by what Vlad was telling me. "Then your name is Vlad the fourth."

"No, there was another Vlad in our family. I am Vlad the fifth."

"Vlad V of the Draculesti royal family." I felt proud.

The End

Thank you for reading my book. If you enjoyed it and would like to help other readers with your comments please write a review on Amazon. And of course I much appreciate your review as well.

For more information about my books please visit **sandru.com**

Or visit me at my website: **sandru.com** and subscribe to my mailing list.

(Your e-mail will not be sold or used for spam)

Follow on stories:

R.I.P., The Death of a Vampire (Vlad V, Bk 2) by Mit Sandru.

Vlad V Draculesti is dying because of an incident that happened decades ago. Unfortunately for Vlad V, the US intelligence agencies investigate him to find out his true identity, and centuries old life. Will Cat Sanders and vampire friends be able to help him die in peace, or will Vlad be discovered for being a vampire and die in a US Federal research laboratory?

Vampire Slayers (Vlad V, Bk 3) by Mit Sandru.

Cat Sanders is a billionaire, but not all is well. Her nemesis, Veronica Seyler, allied with a vampire-slayer drug cult, demands extortion money or she will be killed.

Cat's vampire friend, Angelique, comes to her aid. But the cult is more cunning and dangerous than even her vampire friend could handle. Would Cat and Angelique be able to come out of this alive even if Cat pays the ransom?

Vampires of Transylvania (Vlad V, Bk 4) by Mit Sandru

Cat Sanders has a simple task: spread Vlad V's ashes in Transylvania at midnight, during full moon. But in Transylvania Vlad V has centuries old enemies who take her and her friend Tudor hostage, placing them in iron cages among zombies and proto-vampires. Will they be able to escape from the blood sucking proto-vampires and flesh-eating zombies, or become zombies themselves?

The Queen of Vampires: A New Queen Arises (Vlad V, Bk 5) by Mit Sandru

The Vampire Queen, Eleonore von Schwarzenburg, is bloodthirsty and vengeful on Cat Sanders and her friends. She plans the most painful death for them. Cat and her friends find themselves entrapped and helpless to avoid her wrath.

Will Cat and her friends be able to escape and survive the Queen of Vampires' fury?

Other books:

The Pregnant Pope (TIO Series), by Mit Sandru.

The 92-year-old Pope is pregnant. Although he hasn't undergone any medical procedures, he carries a human fetus in his abdomen. Is this a case of self-cloning, or a mutation? Is this an Immaculate Conception, or Satan's work? Find out how Clair, Travis, and Prescott, the members of the Capuchin Trinity Team, are solving this mystery.

Sferogyls (Timurud Bk. 1) by Mit Sandru

The gods resurrect Tim Andrus from the dead. To his surprise he finds out that he is a god himself, and his name is Timurud.

But, the life of a god is not all heavenly. Timurud must protect weak and powerless civilizations against ferocious galactic empires. His first mission is to defend the peaceful and unarmed Sferogyl race against the Maggotroll Empire, warlike hominids who come to enslave the Sferogyls and capture their planet.

Fighting is the only solution to stay free, but the Sferogyls have no space warships. How will Timurud help them out?

Gold Rush Mystery (Terraspantion Chronicles, Bk. 1) by Mit Sandru.

America is back on the Moon, and we intend to stay and establish a self-sustaining permanent base for tourism and mining. The work is challenging, the environment is deadly, but the astronauts Mia, Geo and Roby succeed in building the moon base, even if they landed in a mysterious crater.

Time Hole, (Terraspantion Chronicles, Bk. 2) by Mit Sandru.

Mining on the moon is a hazardous affair. Deedee and Arno, two lunar generalists, find perils beyond what they signed up for when they travel on the lunar surface at night . . . on the dark side of the Moon. Time will not be the same after they fall into the *Time Hole*.

Folding Reality, by Mit Sandru, a Paranormal, Time Travel Adventure.

Experiencing a new reality is just a paper-fold away for Mike the insurance salesman. But those realities are not by his choice and he ends up being crucified, or gassed at Auschwitz, or marooned in space in a Russian capsule.

Arboregal, the Lorn Tree, by D.G. Sandru.

Four youngsters, Melissa, Perry, Nathan and Michelle materialize in a desolate world where giant, mile-high trees, support all life. They find shelter in the Lorn Tree among the Lorns. Soon after they discover that an evil spirit, Hellferata, wants them dead. Fearful Lorns want to expel the youngsters from their tree, which would be a dead sentence since monsters roam the land at night.

Will their ingenuity, cunning, and courage help them escape, or will Hellferata mete out her wrath before they can escape?

Coloring Book

<u>Abstract Dreams: Coloring Book 1 (Sandru's Art)</u> by Dumitru Sandru

Reward your soul with the smooth and pleasing lines of Abstract Dreams

Non-Fiction, Biography, Political

Escape from Communism, by Dumitru Sandru, a True Story and Commentary.

Life under communism is cruel and inhumane. Communist countries have a "Berlin Wall" around them, and the whole country is a giant concentration camp. I risked my life to escape from hell and reach freedom.

T-Shirts and other stuff:

Sandru's Shop or Sandru's Products

Visit my e-Gallery at:

http://dumitru-sandru.artistwebsites.com/

http://www.artistrising.com/galleries/Sandru

About Dumitru "Mit" Sandru

Dumitru "D.G." "Mit" Sandru was born in the greater area of Transylvania in the last century. He is an artist, composer, and author. He paints in the classical, surreal, and modern styles, and most of the music Dumitru composes is of the New Age flavor. As an author, he prefers to write Science-Fiction, Paranormal, and Teen/Children Fantasy & Sci-Fi novels.

Dumitru resides in California with his wife. They have one daughter and two grandsons.

Visit him at **sandru.com**